D1638804

This book belongs to

_____

Barbie

in

The Snow Palace

Illustrations by Lawrence Mann

EGMONT

EGMONT

We bring stories to life

First published in Great Britain 2009
by Egmont UK Limited
239 Kensington High Street, London W8 6SA

ISBN 978 1 4052 4434 3

45642/2

Printed in Italy

Egmont is passionate about helping to preserve the world's remaining ancient forests.
We only use paper from legal and sustainable forest sources.

This book is made from paper certified by the Forestry Stewardship Council (FSC),
an organisation dedicated to promoting responsible management of forest resources.For more
information on the FSC, please visit www.fsc.org. To learn more about Egmont's sustainable
paper policy, please visit www.egmont.co.uk/ethical

Hello! My name is Krista and I live in a tower filled with wondrous books.

This is what happened when a little snow kitten asked me to help save Snowland from the Ice Queen . . .

One day, Krista was reading in her window seat when it began to snow. Snow was unusual where Krista lived, so she put her book down to watch.

Suddenly, in the flurry of snowflakes, a little kitten floated down in front of her and settled on the windowsill. His fur was as cold as ice!

"Are you lost?" said Krista, opening the window.

"I live in Snowland, but it doesn't seem like home any more," said the snow kitten, sadly. "The Ice Queen has turned it into an unhappy place. Please help us." But before Krista could reply, the kitten was whisked away by a hand made of snowflakes!

Krista knew she had to help the kitten.

Quickly, she went to her bookshelves and searched for stories about Snowland. She read in a huge, blue book that Snowland was full of happy creatures. But the snow kitten had certainly not seemed happy.

"I can't do anything against the Ice Queen," said Krista to herself.

But the moment she said it, she knew it wasn't true. She would have to try!

Early the next morning, Krista took a map and set off for Snowland. The closer she came to Snowland, the colder it became. Even her warmest clothes were too thin. Eventually, she grew so cold and tired that she curled up by the roadside and fell fast asleep.

She was woken by the honking of snowbirds flying overhead. One of them swooped down to ask where she was going. Shyly, Krista told him about the snow kitten and the wicked Ice Queen.

"Good luck!" honked the bird. "Take these feathers, they may come in handy!" He flapped his wings so that soft, downy feathers fluttered into Krista's hands.

As she trudged along, animals came out of their burrows to talk to her.

"The Ice Queen is getting more powerful and the cold is spreading out from Snowland!" growled a white fox cub.

"It used to be warmer here. Now we've nothing to eat!" shivered the hare.

Krista got out her food supplies and shared them with the animals.

"I don't have very much, but I can't let you starve!" she said.

The animals were very grateful. The hare brought her a pair of warm boots and some mittens, and the fox cub said he would come to Snowland with her. He sat on her shoulder and wrapped his tail around her neck for a scarf.

"My name is Ferny," he told her.

"Thank you, Ferny," said Krista. "How far is it to Snowland?" There was so much snow on the ground now that she couldn't tell where she was.

"Ask the reindeer," suggested the fox cub. "He's always on the move. Just follow the hoof prints."

The prints led Krista to a shaggy-coated reindeer. Krista asked him if he knew the way to Snowland.

"Yes, I was born and brought up there," said the reindeer, his shining eyes sorrowful. "I used to run and play on the snow-covered plains, until the Ice Queen banned games."

"Don't worry, I'll speak to the Ice Queen," said Krista, trying to sound brave and confident.

"Then climb on my back and I'll take you to her!" said the reindeer.

They sped away through the freezing night.

Soon they came to a sparkling plain covered in snow crystals. The ice creaked and groaned as they touched the ground.

"Here we are at the edge of Snowland. And look, there's the Ice Queen's palace," said the reindeer, pointing with his nose.

Krista looked up to see the icy pinnacles of the Snow Palace, its towering glass walls glinting in the blue light. They climbed the snowy path. At the top, Krista pushed open the icicle gate, waved goodbye to the reindeer and entered a silent winter garden.

They passed frozen fountains and ice statues, and came to a thorny bush covered in frosted berries.

"Snowberries!" cried Ferny. "They're cold, but tasty."

They ate as much as they wanted, and Krista filled her food bag while snowflakes whirled around them, stinging them. Suddenly the flakes grew bigger and harder, and Krista saw that they had become animals!

"I'm here to help!" she cried. "Ask the snow kitten!"

The snowflake animals stopped attacking and said: "The snow kitten has been held captive by the Queen! She never lets him out of her sight."

They found the Queen seated on her glass throne in the middle of a frozen indoor lake. The snow kitten sat at her feet, on the end of a frosty chain.

"I've come to ask you to free the animals of Snowland from their unhappiness! Please, release the kitten or . . . or . . . !" Suddenly Krista felt afraid. She didn't know what she was doing here. She couldn't fight the Ice Queen!

"I will never set the kitten free!" snapped the Queen, looking down her nose at Krista. "He is my only friend. Now I will turn you into a snowflake!"

The Queen shot a bolt of magic at Krista! But Ferny spread out his bushy tail in front of her face to catch the frosty magic. It fizzled out before Krista's eyes!

Krista was shocked, but suddenly she realised something important. She didn't feel alone and helpless now, because Ferny was her friend. And that gave her an idea about how to help the Queen.

"Wait!" she said to the icy woman. "I've brought you a present."

"No one brings me presents," said the Queen, frostily. "Hmm . . . but show me anyway."

Krista opened her bag and pulled out the snowbird's feathers. An icy wind lifted them up and they fell in a drift around the Queen's shoulders.

The Queen's cheeks turned a rosy pink as she snuggled into the soft, feathery cloak. Her throne melted away as a warm breeze filled the air, and the chain fell from the snow kitten's neck.

"Oh!" she exclaimed, happily. "So this is how it feels to be warm! I never knew."

"Yes," smiled Krista, as Ferny snuggled against her. The snow kitten jumped into the Queen's lap, purring happily as his fur grew warmer.

The Queen stroked the kitten as she said: "Perhaps I have not been a very good queen. But I will think about what you have shown me, Krista. From now on, Snowland will be a better place for everyone."

Krista smiled. She was looking forward to going home and curling up with a book, but there was something she wanted to do first.

"Let's have a snowberry feast!" she said.

So that night there was a party with presents and snowberries for all, and the little snow kitten danced merrily with Ferny. Snowland was a happy place once again!

Magical titles available in this series:

1. The Singing Tree
2. The Jewel Fairies
3. The Ice Dragon
4. The Lost Pearl
5. The Frog Prince
6. Wild Fire
7. Greenfingers' Garden
8. The Firebird
9. The Mystical Moonflower
10. Princess Golden-Hood
11. Misty the Magical Unicorn
12. Fairy Slippers
13. Journey to the Stars
14. The Mermaid's Tail
15. Amelia and the Bear
16. The Rainbow Ark
17. The Goblin King
18. The Northern Lights
19. Unwelcome Guests
20. The Troll's Bridge

Look out for more enchanting tales to add to your collection!